PENGUIN WORKSHOP
Penguin Young Readers Group
An Imprint of Penguin Random House LLC

Library of Congress Control Number: 2018012927

ISBN 9781524787011   10 9 8

www.jessicahische.is/brave

for

Ramona and Charlie

You both inspire me to be my best today, tomorrow, and every day.

TOMORROW
I'LL BE
BRAVE

Words and pictures by

JESSICA HISCHE

Penguin Workshop
An Imprint of Penguin Random House

Tomorrow I'll be

TUROUS

I'll **play** and I'll **explore**

I'll **make** or **learn** or **try** something
I've never done before!

Tomorrow I'll be

STR

I'll **climb** and **jump** and **run**

It doesn't matter if I **win** as long as I **have fun**!

Tomorrow I'll be

I'll **think** before I **act**

I'll **solve** a puzzle, **read** a book,
and **learn** a fun new fact!

fig. 2.

fig. 3.

Tomorrow I'll be

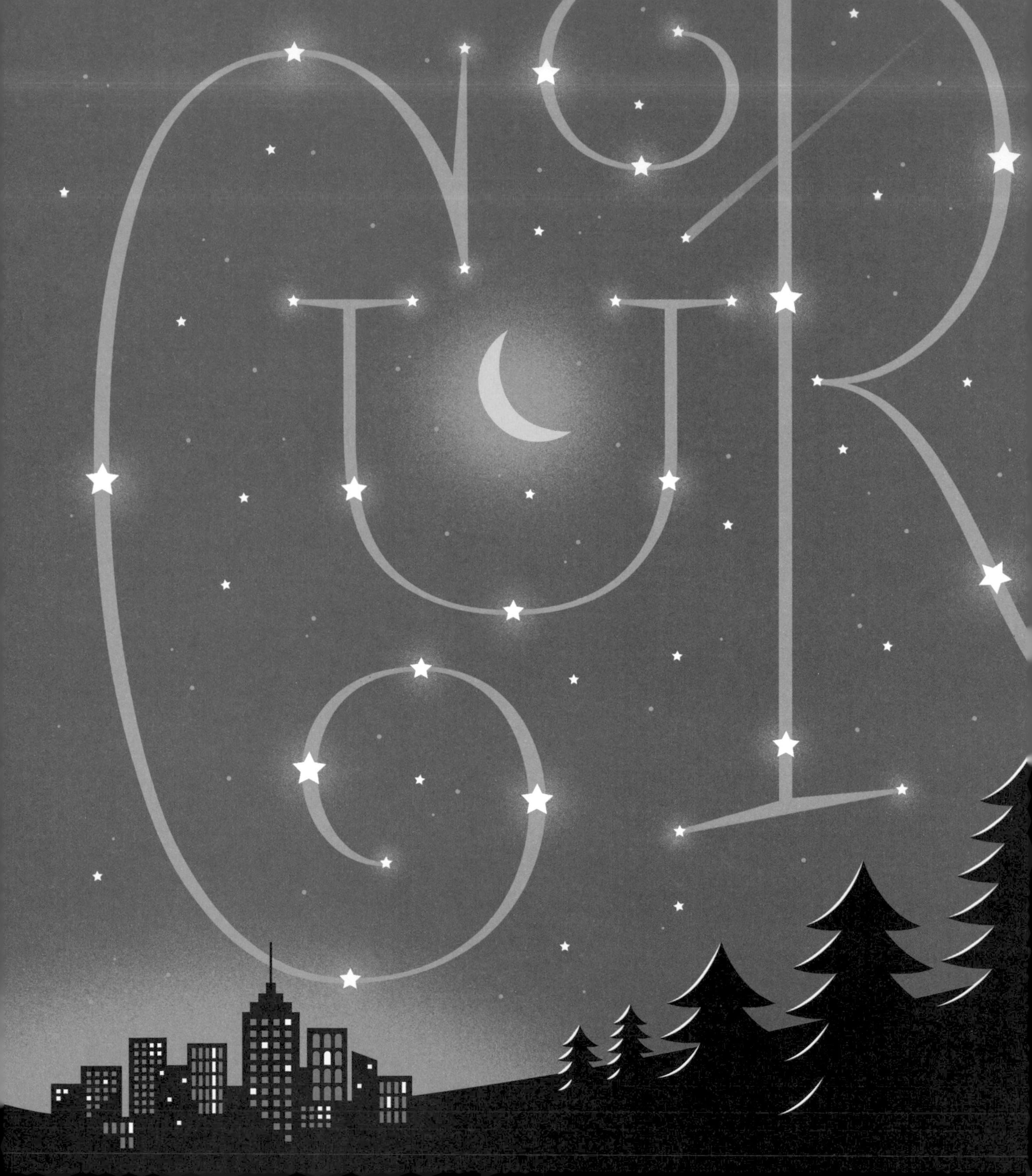

Please **teach** me something new

I'll **ask** why a million times . . .

WHY?

why

Why

WH

WHY?

¿

?

WHY

WARUM

למה?

WHY

Pourquoi

WHY?

WHY

WHY?

WHY?

为什么?

PERCHé

HY

Why

WHY

WHY

~..

WHY

гдуто

왜?

why

¿POR QUÉ?

why

?.

なんで?

. . . maybe a million two.

I'll **color** and **draw** for hours

I'll **play** a game of make-believe
and **use** my magic powers!

Tomorrow I'll be

I'll **be proud** of all I know

I'll **stop** and **smile** and **think** about

how much you've helped me **grow**!

Tomorrow I'll be

There's nothing I can't **do**

I won't **be scared** but if I am
I know that I **have you**.

Tomorrow I'll be all the things
I **tried** to be **today** . . .

ADVENTUROUS

STRONG

SMART

CURIOUS

CREATIVE
CONFIDENT
& BRAVE

and if I wasn't one of them, I know that it's okay.

But **tonight** I'm very sleepy,
so now it's time to **rest**.

Tomorrow I'll be all these things
or at least **I'll try my best.**

ADVENTUROUS STRONG SMART